Bedtime Poems
Moonlight Rhymes

To Steve and Nicky

Compiled by Mary Joslin
This edition copyright © 2004 Lion Hudson
Illustrations copyright © 1997 Liz Pichon
Design by Nicky Jex

The author asserts the moral right
to be identified as the author of this work

A Lion Children's Book
an imprint of
Lion Hudson plc
Mayfield House, 256 Banbury Road,
Oxford OX2 7DH, England
www.lionhudson.com
ISBN 0 7459 4897 9

First hardback edition 1997
First paperback edition 2004
1 3 5 7 9 10 8 6 4 2 0

A catalogue record for this book is available from the British Library

Printed and bound in Singapore

Acknowledgments

We would like to thank all those who have given us permission to include
quotations in this book. Every effort has been made to trace and acknowledge
copyright holders. We apologize for any errors or omissions that may remain,
and would ask those concerned to contact the publishers, who will ensure that
full acknowledgment is made in the future.

'Silver' by Walter de la Mare reproduced by permission of
The Literary Trustees of Walter de la Mare, and The Society
of Authors as their representative.
'Sun is shining', 'Climb a silver ladder', 'Dear God, you are
my shepherd' and 'Dear God, look from your heaven' by Lois Rock,
reproduced by permission of the author.

LION
CHILDREN'S

Bedtime Poems
Moonlight Rhymes

Compiled by Mary Joslin
Illustrated by Liz Pichon

God bless all those that I love;

God bless all those that love me:

God bless all those that love those that I love

and all those that love those that love me.

Contents

Day is done,

Gone the sun

From the lake,

From the hills,

From the sky.

Safely rest,

All is well!

God is nigh.

Part 1
Day is over

'O dandelion, yellow as gold,
What do you do all day?'

'I just wait here in the tall green grass
Till the children come to play.'

'O dandelion, yellow as gold,
What do you do all night?'

'I wait and wait till the cool dews fall
And my hair grows long and white.'

'And what do you do when your hair is white
And the children come to play?'

'They take me up in their dimpled hands
And blow my hair away!'

Over in the meadow
By a pond in the sun
Lived an old mother duck
And her little duckie one.
'Quack,' said the mother,
'We quack,' said the one.
And they quacked and were happy
By the pond in the sun.

Over in the meadow
Where the stream runs blue
Lived an old mother fish
And her baby fishes two.
'Swim,' said the mother,
'We swim,' said the two,
And they swam and were happy
Where the stream runs blue.

Over in the meadow
In a nest in a tree
Lived an old mother sparrow
And her hatchlings three.
'Sing,' said the mother,
'We sing,' said the three,
And they sang and were happy
In their nest in a tree.

Over in the meadow
On the mud by the shore
Lived an old mother frog
And her little froggies four.
'Hop,' said the mother,
'We hop,' said the four,
And they hopped and were happy
On the mud by the shore.

Over in the meadow
In a straw beehive
Lived an old mother queenbee
And her honey bees five.
'Hum,' said the queen,
'Hmmm, hmmm,' said the five,
And they hummed and were happy
In their straw beehive.

Over in the meadow
In the evening sun
Danced a pretty mother
And her baby one.
'Look,' said the mother,
'At the ducks and the bees,
At the frogs and the fish
And the birds in the trees.'

'We hum,' said the five,

'We hop,' said the four,

'We sing,' said the three,

'We swim,' said the two,

'Quack, quack,' said the one,

And they all played together

Till the day was done.

Who has seen
the wind?
Neither I nor you:
But when the leaves
hang trembling
The wind is passing
through.

Who has seen

the wind?

Neither you nor I:

But when the trees

bow down their heads

The wind is passing by.

Christina Rossetti

Boats sail on
the rivers,
And ships sail
on the seas;

But clouds that
sail across the sky
Are prettier far
than these.

There are bridges
on the rivers,
As pretty
as you please;

But the bow that bridges heaven,
  And overtops the trees,
  And builds a road from earth to sky,
    Is prettier far than these.

CHRISTINA ROSSETTI

Little drops of water,
Little grains of sand,
Make the mighty ocean,
And the pleasant land.

Little deeds of kindness,
Little words of love,
Make this earth an Eden
Like the heaven above.

ISAAC WATTS

Sun is shining
all for you:
Paint your sky
a sunny blue.

Rain and showers
are on their way:
Paint your sky
in shades of grey.

22

North wind blows
with all its might:
Paint your clouds
with swirls of white.

Day is over,
time for bed:
Paint your sky
with gold and red.

LOIS ROCK

Now the day is over,
    Night is drawing nigh,
Shadows of the evening
    Steal across the sky.

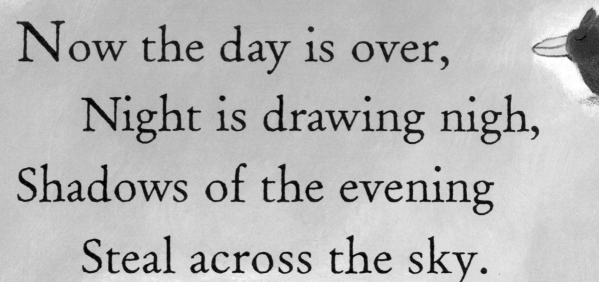

Now the darkness gathers,
Stars begin to peep,
Birds and beasts and flowers
Soon will be asleep.

S. BARING-GOULD

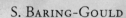

Climb a silver ladder
To the moon above.
Pick a bowl of starlight
For the one you love.

LOIS ROCK

Part 2
Moon and stars

All day long
The sun shines bright.
The moon and stars
Come out by night.
From twilight time
They line the skies
And watch the world
With quiet eyes.

Star light, star bright,
First star I see tonight,
I wish I may, I wish I might,
Have the wish I wish tonight.

The sun descending in the west,
The evening star does shine,
The birds are silent in their nest,
And I must seek for mine.

The moon, like a flower,
In heaven's high bower,
With silent delight
Sits and smiles on the night.

WILLIAM BLAKE

The moon shines clear as silver, The sun shines bright like gold, And both are very lovely, And very, very old.

God hung them up as lanterns, For all beneath the sky; And nobody can blow them out, For they are up too high.

CHARLOTTE DRUITT COLE

33

Silver

Slowly, silently, now the moon
Walks the night in her silver shoon;
This way, and that, she peers, and sees
Silver fruit upon silver trees;
One by one the casements catch
Her beams beneath the silvery thatch;
Couched in his kennel, like a log,
With paws of silver sleeps the dog;
From their shadowy cote the white breasts peep
Of doves in a silver-feathered sleep;
A harvest mouse goes scampering by,
With silver claws, and silver eye;
And moveless fish in the water gleam,
By silver reeds in a silver stream.

WALTER DE LA MARE

Twinkle, twinkle,
little star,
How I wonder
what you are!
Up above the
world so high,
Like a diamond
in the sky.

When the
blazing sun is gone,
When he nothing
shines upon,
Then you show your
little light,
Twinkle, twinkle,
all the night.

Then the traveller
in the dark,
Thanks you for
your tiny spark,
He could not see
which way to go,
If you did not
twinkle so.

As your bright
and tiny spark,
Lights the traveller
in the dark,—
Though I know not
what you are,
Twinkle, twinkle,
little star.

JANE TAYLOR

Go to sleep, my darling,
Close your pretty eyes.
Angels up above you
Peep down from the skies.

Part 3
Lullaby

Wee Willie Winkie
    runs through the town,
Upstairs and downstairs
    in his night-gown,

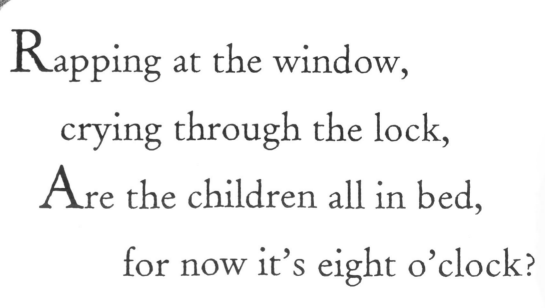

Rapping at the window,
    crying through the lock,
Are the children all in bed,
    for now it's eight o'clock?

Little lambs, little lambs,
Where do you sleep?
'In the green meadow,
With mother sheep.'

Little birds, little birds,
Where do you rest?
'Close to our mother,
In a warm nest.'

Baby dear, Baby dear,
Where do you lie?
'In my warm bed,
With Mother close by.'

A wise old owl lived in an oak;

The more he saw

the less he spoke;

The less he spoke

the more he heard.

Why can't we all be like

that wise old bird?

There were three little owls in a wood

who sang hymns whenever they could;

What the words were about

One could never make out,

But one felt it was doing them good.

Sweet dreams, form a shade
O'er my lovely infant's head:

Sweet dreams of pleasant streams
By happy, silent, moony beams.

WILLIAM BLAKE

Hush! my dear, lie still and slumber;
Holy Angels guard thy bed!
Heavenly blessings without number
Gently falling on thy head.

ISAAC WATTS

I see the moon,
And the moon sees me;
God bless the moon,
And God bless me.

Part 4
Safe this night

Lord, when we have not any light,
And mothers are asleep,
Then through the stillness of the night
Thy little children keep.

When shadows haunt the quiet room,
Help us to understand
That thou art with us through the gloom,
To hold us by the hand.

ANNE MATHESON

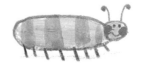

Dear Father, hear and bless
Thy beasts and singing birds,

And guard with tenderness,
    Small things that have no words.

Jesus, friend of little children
Be a friend to me;
Take my hand and ever keep me
Close to thee.

Dear God, you are my shepherd,
You give me all I need,
You take me where the grass grows green
And I can safely feed.

You take me where the water
    Is quiet and cool and clear;
And there I rest and know I'm safe
    For you are always near.

LOIS ROCK, BASED ON PSALM 23

Dear God, look from your heaven
Upon my boat and me,
Protect me from the billows
Of the great and stormy sea.

LOIS ROCK

Lord, keep us safe this night,
Secure from all our fears;

May angels guard us while we sleep,
Till morning light appears.

JOHN LELAND

The moon shines bright,
The stars give light
Before the break of day;
God bless you all
Both great and small
And send a joyful day.

Index of first lines